THE Cat THAT Overcame

Original title: Pinky

by HELEN LA PENTA

Illustrated by Taylor Oughton

Scholastic Book Services
New York   Toronto   London   Auckland   Sydney

To my brother
Mario La Penta

Cover by Hans Reinhard / Bruce Coleman Incorporated

ISBN: 0-590-10333-4

12 11 10 9 8 7   0 1/8

Printed in Canada by Webcom Limited

1

"It's an honest working cat," Sadie said. "If you've got a barn it will work there."

"Our barn is used for a garage," said Mrs. Colby. "But I'll take it just to please you, Sadie. Pinky? What a funny name."

Sadie wanted to tell Mrs. Colby not to do that. Nobody should take an animal unless he was really wanted for himself. That's what Sadie thought. But it had been so hard to find a place for this last (and homeliest) of the litter that she did not have the heart to object. The Higginses down the road would be glad she had found a home for their unwanted runt. "People considered him," she had said to Dan yesterday morning when she brought him home, "but they thought he'd die on their hands."

"That cat won't die," Cap'n Dan had declared shortly after turning a sailor's weather eye on the scrap of tiger cat fur that was Pinky. "How'd they come to call him Pinky?" he asked.

"Children named him," Sadie told him. "On account of his nose being so pink and there not being much else to him."

"Got a nice little white stripe just pointing to that pink nose, too," Dan said. "Just like an arrow which says: 'See this? That's my name: Pinky.'"

"Mrs. Higgins wouldn't let them keep him. One cat is enough, she says. And Mr. Thomas wouldn't have him for the Christmas party."

"Anyway," Sadie thought now as she closed the door on Mrs. Colby and Pinky, "it will be a long time before that cat catches anything more 'n a cold. He might as well have a home for whatever reason, though the Colbys haven't been in these parts long enough — eight, maybe nine years, seems — for anybody to know what they're really like."

She watched the car turning on the wet road with the sleet and the rain hitting it head on.

Then she looked up at the black, scowling skies glowering over Cape Cod. What a morning it was! Not a scrap of comfort in it anywhere. Before going back to the stove she looked out the other window, which faced east, and watched the whitecaps out to sea. Time was when there were fewer trees and a body could see clear to the end of nowhere. But now all these newfangled cottages being put up, and motels, and cabins, and what-have-you — and trees growing all the time. Things were changing all up and down the Cape. That was a fact.

"Sea's rough," she called out to Dan who sat at the opposite window, on the road side.

"Eh-ya," said Dan quietly. He was watching a bluebird swinging himself on the very top of a low juniper. That bird acted just as if he were sitting in a rocker. "Got to have feathers for this weather," Dan told Sadie. Then he turned to look at her and added, "You know we're going to see that cat back, don't you?"

"I reckon," Sadie agreed.

Pinky had an idea he wasn't too well liked, so he hastily found a place for himself under the Colby living room couch.

"Get that cat out of there," said Mr. Colby who was reading a copy of the *Cape Codder* he had brought home that morning. "He'll do something."

Mrs. Colby got a broom and pushed Pinky out. "Scat!" she said irritably. "I wonder why I ever took him!"

"That's what I'd like to know," said Mr. Colby just as irritably. "I've never liked cats and you know it. He looks homely enough to scare mice."

"That might not be a bad idea. If we had mice. Sadie had him left over — or the Higginses, neighbors down the road, did — and she couldn't find a place for him. I — I thought I'd help her out. She's such a sweet old thing. She and Dan are first cousins, did you know? His children are all married, and she's all alone. The house belonged to both their mothers, so there they are."

"Fine! But I still don't want that cat."

While this conversation was going on Pinky found himself another place, under the table this time. He looked around, misery stamped all over him. He tried miaowing — and continued trying — but he was too frightened to get any sound out. His mouth kept opening and closing and he alternately shut and opened his eyes as well. It was plain that he would rather not see what he was seeing.

Mrs. Colby said, "He ought to be in a house where there are children. But even Mr. Thomas — you know, the Episcopal church in Orleans — wouldn't have him. Too sickly looking for the Christmas party — where you can give away almost anything. Going to give kittens away in Christmas stockings."

"Well, he's no beauty. He looks mangy," Mr. Colby said.

"He's all right as far as that goes," said his wife. "Just small — skin and bones — the runt of the litter, Sadie said. He looks all eyes."

"Looks like a truck driver. Hey, you!" Mr. Colby snapped his fingers, and Pinky blinked back. He opened and shut his mouth but couldn't get any of that awful feeling out of him. For some reason this amused Mr. Colby and he chuckled.

"What do you mean — truck driver?" Mrs. Colby was puzzled.

"He looks battered even though he's just born."

Mrs. Colby shrugged her shoulders. She saw not the least resemblance between that handful of cat fur and a truck driver. And why should a truck driver be battered anyway?

"Look, honey," Mr. Colby said in a reasonable tone of voice, "I don't like him. I don't want him around — just don't like cats. See if you can find him a place where there are children."

Mrs. Colby picked up the cat and ran out to the garage with him. She wished she had never stopped in to see Sadie that morning.

2

Pinky, left alone in the garage, called out once or twice. It was damp and cold and there was nothing but the concrete floor to sit on, but he was less frightened than when strangers were around. He made a sound. It was low and it quivered, but it came out.

He sniffed here and there cautiously, looked up at the two dusty windows which he could not reach, made as if to sit down, took a few steps forward and stood there considering. All the time the rain drummed on the garage roof and the wind made a who-o-o-ah-oh sound as it went by.

In a corner some strands of twine looked suspicious. Pinky went over and took a few half-hearted swipes at them. Then he called out with a loud, unhappy voice and listened. There was no answer. He was a small cat. The cement floor was cold. The air was damp. And that was all there was to the world. These are the things he said in that prolonged cry, but there was no one to hear him.

A sudden burst of energy beckoned him toward the far side as if he had received some marvelous information. And perhaps he had, because after scuttling beneath the shiny new car he came upon an old, battered one, and glancing up saw something promising — the running board, which was something the new car did not have. It was exactly high enough for him to reach with one leap, and he hopped on it. Careful inspection was encouraging: it was not as cold as the floor. He tucked his paws under him and settled down to that relaxed wait-and-see attitude that belongs to a cat as surely as his whiskers. Life was short of comfort — but only at the moment. He would wait. Perhaps he would sleep. Once or twice he lifted his head, opened his eyes, and sent a plaintive mew into the coldness. Then with quivers and twitches he settled himself more and more into himself, becoming very small, so that the cold should have as little as possible of him. In a minute he was indistinguishable from the color of the running board. His little nose, which had lost most of its pinkness, sank lower and lower until it was no more than a whisker's breadth from the running board.

Pinky slept his troubles away.

When the garage door opened suddenly he took one frantic leap, landed on the cement floor, arched his back, and spat with mighty cat fury. There were two enormous, dark shadows in the doorway, and they would catch it from him if they dared come a step nearer.

They had a great deal of courage, and did.

One of them turned out to be a large man who smelled of fish and tobacco, and who caught him in one of his powerful hands before Pinky had a chance to defend himself (or even make a wild dash for freedom). Pinky spat, and spat again, then, finding this useless, he blinked sullenly at the large face beneath a black and red cap.

"Put him in a box and drop him in the pond," said the man. "Take him out of his misery."

"Ugh! I couldn't do that, Mr. Ransler," said Mrs. Colby. "You do it for me."

"Going out clamming if this weather ever lets up," said Mr. Ransler. "Do it then." He dropped Pinky into a burlap bag he was carrying. "Meantime I'll let him stay at home with the Missus a day — see if the kids fancy him and if she'll let them keep him. If she does, there's the shed out in back 'n he can stay there."

"You do that," said Mrs. Colby, thoroughly glad to be rid of the cat.

Pinky scrambled desperately up the sides of the sack and Mr. Ransler gave the bag a shake that fairly rattled Pinky's few teeth and his empty insides. He could hear the wind and the rain and sleet slap at the sack as Mr. Ransler walked to the car; then he felt himself dropped on a hard surface, though warmer and softer than concrete. There was an agreeable odor of fish all around him, and if *only* there had been something to eat he was sure he would have felt better. Instead, there was a terrible explosion not far from him,and pretty soon he was being shaken and tossed, as whatever he was on or in jogged along throwing him from side to side.

Life was terrifying.

3

Pinky thought he would die. Then he was sure he would. He was lifted up suddenly and was so sick he was past caring. All at once he was as limp as the sack itself.

Somewhere around him he knew there was rain and wind — all that awful stuff that lives outside a house — but in a minute it turned into indoor warmth, and he was set down on a hard surface.

"Don't put that dirty bag on my nice clean kitchen table," said Mrs. Ransler. "What's in it?"

"A cat."

"Cat?" Mrs. Ransler's voice held surprise and

a tinge of horror. She put the bag down on the floor.

"Where's the cat?" said Lyle, who was six. He came stomping into the kitchen on a pair of make-believe lion's feet and was about to reach for the bag when his older sister stopped him.

"Let Daddy open it," she said with authority.

But Jean, who was not quite three, came in at that moment and threw herself on top of the bag.

"Poor cat!" Mrs. Ransler hastily pulled the baby off.

Pinky, who had considered himself as good as smothered less than a minute ago, promptly started clawing his way to freedom as soon as Mr. Ransler opened the bag. Unfortunately, the baby's hand was still close enough for him to claw it, and in half a second the house was in an uproar. The baby screamed, the mother shouted, the father scolded, the two older children yelled, and Pinky found himself clutched in Mr. Ransler's iron hand once again.

"Here, I'll put him out in the shed. Going to drown him anyway," Mr. Ransler said.

This started the older children pleading for him.

"You can't keep him," Mrs. Ransler said firmly. "I've got problems enough without a cat. Anyway, look at him. He's the ugliest little cat I ever saw. If we're going to get a cat let's get a really pretty one at the pet shop in Hyannis."

"But, Mom," said Beth, the older girl, "maybe he'd grow up to be nice-looking."

"Wouldn't live's more like it," said her father, and started walking toward the back door, clutching Pinky in his big fist.

"Give him some warm milk at least," cried Lyle. "Please, Mom, give him some warm milk."

"All right, son," his mother said, "I'll give him some warm milk. But now let your father take him out to the shed. I'll bring him the milk in a minute."

The shed was colder and darker than the garage but at least it had a wooden floor, which was a little softer than concrete, and didn't rattle and shake like the other thing he had been in. The wind blew in through cracks, lots of them, some quite large enough for Pinky to slip through if he had wanted. There was a doll carriage with a soft mattress and a flannel blanket which might have been a great comfort to him. But he was too sick and too frightened to realize he might

14

escape, and he was too small to reach the soft flannel blanket inside the doll carriage.

Mrs. Ransler kept her promise. She came out with a flashlight and put a saucer of warm milk beside him. He edged away instantly, but after she had gone he went up to it cautiously. First he stuck both his paws in the saucer, then he shook them, then he sat down and licked them, then he went back and stuck his nose right down into the milk and wheezed and sneezed. But at last he set to, and for a long time he was busy lapping and shivering. When he found enough energy to give himself a proper wash, he began to feel more like himself again. He miaowed once or twice tentatively, but he knew there would be no answer. Perhaps as he stood there, feeling the great lonesomeness of this new dark place, he thought of Sadie's and Dan's big, comfortable kitchen where he had spent a whole day and night. Perhaps he thought how snug he had been, sheltered against the thick fur of his mother's body, surrounded by his strong brothers and sisters, and how they all tumbled over each other. And perhaps he did not think at all, and only knew that he was alone and unwanted, though slightly less wretched than he had been a short time ago.

High up there was one small window. He could see the night and the rain through it. After thinking about it for some time, he began to edge carefully in its direction. A big rubber ball came rolling past him. He gave it a swipe and moved out of its way. Then his paws touched softness and he started kneading, giving little purring gasps of contentment. It was a corduroy jacket that had fallen from a nail against the wall. It had a lovely smell. Things could be worse. Pinky settled himself in its folds and slept.

In the middle of the night — or so it seemed to Pinky — the large, iron grip had him again, and quite as suddenly as it had found him it plunged him into a small enclosure.

If he had not been so tired from his struggle to stay alive, he would have heard the shed door open and the two sets of footsteps coming toward him.

"You had better go before the children wake up," said Mrs. Ransler. "Tie the box up good."

Pinky was tossed about as Mr. Ransler tied the box. "It's only five o'clock and pitch black. I'll have some breakfast first," said Mr. Ransler.

"Guess you better," said his wife. "You need

something to stick to your ribs in this weather. Cranberry Bog Pond's frozen over. Where you going to chuck it?"

"Take it to Snow's Landing and throw it off from the little jetty. Tide'll be coming in an hour from now — come drifting back, likely, but then there's always muck settling back. I'll give it a good heave."

"Such bother!" said Mrs. Ransler. "I hope Mrs. Colby remembers to buy her fish off us 'stead of the Portuguese."

"Always good to do folks a favor," said Mr. Ransler, "whether she buys it off us, or don't."

Then Pinky was alone again. The box was small and it was hard to breathe. He was dead certain he was in for really bad trouble this time, though he didn't know of what kind. He turned from one end of his tiny prison to the other searching for an opening. There was nothing — just nothing! It was a fairly sturdy box and, considering its purpose, Mr. Ransler had not thought it necessary to punch holes in it. The water would soak through soon enough, he reasoned, and send it to the bottom.

After a while Pinky felt himself being picked up in his box, carried somewhere, and dropped.

Then came the same awful explosion and the jogging and tossing that said nothing to him, except that terror was being piled on terror and torment.

And then the most dreadful thing yet happened — he was flying through the air, and his hair stood on end, and he spread his claws to grasp at something, but there was nothing to grasp at because he could not leap and he could not see beyond the four narrow cardboard walls in which he was shut up.

Smack! Swish-slosh! His prison came down on something hard. He hit his head, his insides rattled, and for a time he had no consciousness of anything at all.

Mr. Ransler watched the box a minute as it floated on the water.

"Doggone!" he muttered. "Wind was agin' me, but won't take long for the water to soak through 'fore the box comes ashore — if it does. More likely it'll sink half way over."

"Hey, Ransler!" a voice called from the road.

"Hi, Chuck! Rain's gone anyhow, ain't it?" Mr. Ransler greeted his friend, and they drove off together in Ransler's car.

4

The box went bobbing up and down on the waters of Nauset Harbor. The sun was just topping the horizon in the direction of Provincetown. As it rose the wind started blowing at a good, stiff clip, crisping the waters of the incoming tide.

Inside the box it was getting wetter and wetter, though Pinky knew nothing of it. Up and down, up and down went the box as the tide hurried shoreward now, and the waves mounted to their white crests and descended to their gold and russet and purple gullies, carrying along the cardboard box with its light cargo. Streaks of green, that told how cold the water was, looked like lean, green arms, pushing it toward shore. Then a white cap would retrieve it for its own ocean life. Sometimes the box spun like a top before it reached another summit. Slowly it settled into the cold waters. It was halfway under when a broad, green comber gave it a mighty heave that sent it scraping bottom close to the tide line. The next wave swept over it. Salt sea water rained down on Pinky as the box rolled back into the sea and he took a couple of blind, desperate licks at his shoulder. At that moment a gust of wind and a wave together gave the box a final shove and deposited it with the driftwood against the rim of the tide.

Dazed, wet, and trembling, Pinky twisted himself first one way then the other in his narrow prison, and this time his sharp claws worked through the wet cardboard. Something golden pierced through the slit at one corner that his claws had opened. The slit was little wider than one of his whiskers, but it helped him breathe. With the persistence that only the descendant of a mouse-catching family can know, Pinky scratched and tore and pushed at the spot until his whiskers got through. Then he got his nose

out, then one ear, and one eye, and the other eye and ear, and one shoulder, and the other shoulder. Finally, with both paws out, he clawed at the unstable sand and continued to claw at it until his hind legs were out. At last his tail came triumphantly free and he swished it in defiance of all indignity and trouble!

He sat down on the sand and washed himself, stopping occasionally to cast a baleful eye at this great, golden something in the sky that was staring him in the face so rudely. After a while he stopped long enough to consider the premises on which he stood. He surveyed them with cool, critical, and remorseless green eyes, and with the barest minimum of optimism. Having assured himself that this was no paradise but better than a prison by a whole lot, he proceeded with his washing. He tried to shake the sand out of his wet legs, and he tried licking it off. Distasteful stuff! He scowled at the sun again. There was really no end to trouble. But as he blinked his eyes against the brilliant and gentle warmth, a sense of well-being came right through his wet fur to his slow-beating heart. He sniffed gratefully. He was being wrapped in a grand, snug, golden overcoat that was a real comfort, and he began to wash whiskers and ears with a sudden feeling that things were mending and there was a chance he might get out of all this mess before long. He stretched out his lean neck and looked off in the distance and all round him. There were miles and miles and miles of the awful stuff. You couldn't move a paw without being sucked down into it.

A flock of slim birds went about on quick, long legs, making funny marks on the sand. Overhead larger birds circled and swooped and called to each other with echoing, sharp cries. One of them dived down almost low enough to touch him. Pinky somehow knew he was in no danger from him and that the gull was only looking him over, but he ducked anyhow.

A wave came swishing up, depositing foam next to his damp tail, and he jumped back and started walking up the beach with uncertain steps until he came to a dark object. It was a boot, partly torn at the top, and the opening faced the rising sun. Pinky inspected it carefully, sniffing all round it and craning his thin neck to survey the other side. Then, gingerly, he settled himself in it, and while the sun dried his fur and warmed him he slept the sleep of those who have bravely fought and won.

When he awoke the sun was high overhead. He emerged slowly from his shelter, stretching and yawning. There were no birds overhead now, the wind had died down, and he was dry. He looked in the direction of the water, then toward the trees, and on a sudden impulse started walking landward on legs that were a little less shaky than they had been.

Just about this time Bill the iceman was delivering ice at the Nickersons, which was the house closest to Snow's Landing. As he came out he was thinking of his next stop, which was Cap'n Dan's and Sadie's house around the bend of Champlain Road. He looked over his shoulder to see if Nate had come by to chop down that tree for Sadie. She claimed it shut off her view and she couldn't abide trees that stood between her and a clear view of Nauset Harbor. Such a condition brought out her one cranky streak, and since Nate hadn't been yet, Bill prepared himself to hear from Sadie about this — at length.

The truck had been parked on the blacktop road across from the Nickersons, right on the edge of the dunes, and as he was about to step into it again, he thought he saw something moving along the beach. He looked again. It was a bedraggled gray kitten. "Looks like he needs a hand," said Bill to himself. With two jumps he was on him and had the spitting mite in the palm of his hand. "Where do you think you're going?" he asked, grinning.

Pinky did not know why but the voice was immensely reassuring. He stopped spitting, put out his small nose and rubbed it against one of Bill's fingers. Bill made that funny laughing sound in his throat again and said, "Take you over to Cap'n Dan and Sadie, I will. Old Sadie'll find a place for you, chick."

In answer Pinky got out a cracked and wheezy miao, began to purr, and sneezed.

"Gasundheit!" said Bill.

When he got back to his truck he put Pinky on the seat beside him, and whistled for his dog Doyle while he went back of the truck to pick up something he had left there.

Doyle, who had been patrolling the pinewood at the side of the road (which was what he usually did when he and Bill stopped at the Nickersons), came bounding back and leaped to his seat. When he saw the kitten he barked madly. He would not have hurt a hair of Pinky's head, because Doyle was the kindest of dogs and was used to cats, kittens, and most of the critters that lived on the Cape. It was just that he had been taken by surprise. But Pinky, who did not know this, and knew nothing whatever about Doyle, took a flying leap out of the open window, landed on four paws by some miracle, and ran into the woods.

"Hey, you, Doyle!" Bill shouted at him, and ran after Doyle, who had run after Pinky. But the kitten was gone.

A skunk along his path became unnerved by the flying ball of cat fur and squirted at him. Fortunately for Pinky he missed him, and with the strength of desperation Pinky managed to climb a fledgling pine and crouched, more dead than alive, where the first branches forked. If Doyle could have managed to pass the skunk odor barrier he could have reached him with no trouble at all, but he had had skunk trouble once in his life and was taking no chances. The air was so thick with skunk odor that Doyle turned back in disgust and Bill called, "Kitty, kitty!" from a good, safe distance. He soon had to acknowledge the uselessness of this and they went back to the truck.

"Darned you, Doyle!" he said to his dog as he put in his clutch. "What'd you scare him for?

You're used to cats." Doyle looked crest-fallen and neither of them spoke until Bill gave him a rough pat and said, "My fault." Doyle looked happier.

Sadie and Dan had a lot of callers that afternoon. One of them was Steve Venna who had a composition to write and had chosen as his title, "Ships that Sank in Cape Waters." He thought Dan might help him with it.

"You've got a mighty ambitious title there," said Cap'n Dan. "Could go on writing for quite a spell on it — so many of 'em." But he obliged by telling Steve, who was in first-year high, about some of the rescue work he had engaged in during his many years with the Coast Guard. As he talked, he whittled.

"Do you always whittle?" Steve asked.

"Pretty near — when I'm yarnin'."

"Guess that's why they call you Cap'n Dan the Jacknife Man."

"I reckon."

After a while Steve got something to whittle at, too, but just what he was making he wasn't sure. Cap'n Dan was making a surfboat.

Steve was just leaving when old Mr. Cummings — Scotch bonnet on his head and tailor's needle in his lapel, to keep everybody straight on his nationality and trade—came along to leave Dan and Sadie a copy of the *Cape Codder* and to pass the time of day.

Then, about the time that Bill and Doyle were getting back in the truck after their unsuccessful attempt to retrieve Pinky, Mrs. Frazer came knocking at Sadie's door. She had been there earlier to pass the time of day on her way to town, and shortly after leaving had discovered that the diamond on her engagement ring had dropped out of its setting, so she was back to have a look round Sadie's kitchen floor in the hope of finding it there. Before Sadie had time to open the door, though, she had seen the diamond twinkling up at her from the gravel at her feet, below the two shallow steps that led inside.

"I've found it! Sadie, I've found it!" she exclaimed excitedly, holding it in the palm of her hand and laughing.

Sober-eyed as always, Sadie asked, "Are you sure it's yours?"

From his corner by the window Dan heard this scrap of conversation between the two ladies. His eyes and ears and wits were keen and quick, even if he was pushing ninety. "Ain't nobody sowing diamonds outside our door as I know of, Sadie," he called out.

Sadie and Mrs. Frazer were still at the door talking when Bill and Doyle came up the walk. Doyle, sure of his welcome at this house, gave Sadie a wag, and stepped past her politely but firmly for a visit with Cap'n Dan.

Bill put the cake of ice in Sadie's neat icebox.

"Hear Josh's still hauling in lobsters, storm or no," Dan said, conversationally.

"Ma got a real corker from him — was yesterday — weighed near three pounds," Bill agreed. "Only man on the Cape that fetches 'em, storm or no."

"Bide a while?" Sadie sat down facing the window and rocked.

Bill took a chair next to the stove, where Doyle sprawled in comfort, and lit his pipe. Though Bill was no more than twenty-two himself, he always enjoyed stopping off for a chat with Dan and Sadie. They were very distant cousins of his.

"I was bringing you a kitten," he said, looking at both of them over the flame of the match.

"Only the other day found a home for one," said Sadie. "Gave it to those new people at Brewster, the Colbys."

"Was a nice little cat — tiger," put in Dan, "not much to look at but spunky for his size."

"Tiger?" Bill said, taking the pipe out of his mouth. "One I found on the beach this afternoon was a tiger, too. Doyle here barked him off. Not his fault. I forgot he didn't know him."

"Where was that?" asked Sadie.

"Up by Nickerson's — Snow's Landing."

"Couldn't be the same one," Sadie said.

"Or it could. Folks you don't know much about act so many different ways you never thought on," Dan said.

Bill shook his head doubtfully. "Brewster's a long way from Snow's Landing."

"If Dan says it could be Pinky, it's likely," Sadie said, rocking herself.

"Sadie and me's cousins," Cap'n Dan informed Bill. "Daughter to my own mother's sister."

This remark would have sounded strange and out of place to anyone else, especially since Bill of course knew Dan and Sadie were cousins — had known it all his life — but young as he was, Bill understood a lot and he knew this was Dan's way of explaining Sadie's loyalty to him.

"No bigger'n a minute," Bill said, looking at Dan. "Ran off into the woods."

"If you don't mind," Sadie said, "I'd like to drive out with you, Bill. Could be, if he heard my voice, and it is Pinky, he'd come."

"He scared a skunk, I guess, and there's a pretty strong smell, Sadie."

"Well, we can call anyhow."

It was a fine winter afternoon cold and clear, and the sea at Nauset Harbor showed hardly a ripple. With no wind at all the skunk odor had settled down to stay. It was still much too powerful for Doyle and he would not get out of the truck. But Sadie and Bill went bravely forward into the underbrush a little way, and called "Puss-puss-puss!" and "Kitty-kitty-kitty!"

At last they turned back and Doyle was glad to see they had that much sense.

"Won't live — was all bones, and too young to be on his own," Bill declared as they got back in the truck.

"If it's Pinky," Sadie said, "Dan thinks he will live." That seemed to settle the matter for her, but as they drove away her narrow, wrinkled face was sad, and she looked back several times.

5

Pinky heard Bill and Sadie calling "Puss-puss-puss!" and "Kitty-kitty-kitty!" but by that time he was a long way from the tree he had climbed. There was something familiar about those voices, particularly one of them. Both spoke to him comfortingly, but he was too busy disentangling himself from briars and jumping over obstacles to turn their way.

To put as much distance as he could between himself and the skunk smell, he had had to get out of that tree somehow, and after many tries had finally managed to tumble down. The bed of pine needles below it was soft and fragrant but a chipmunk chattered at him and Pinky jumped, spit, and ran in the opposite direction. When he realized the odor increased, he turned tail, ran past the chipmunk who was still scolding him, until both skunk smell and chipmunk were left far behind.

For a small cat who had had nothing more than a saucer of milk the night before, had nearly perished by drowning that morning, had set himself free from a box prison by his own unaided strength, and had escaped the jaws of a large, unknown animal by climbing his first tree, Pinky was doing pretty well.

There wasn't much time to examine things as carefully as he would have done had circumstances been different. At one point he fell into a small hollow and was nearly smothered by damp leaves. He scrambled out and briars caught at his fur, and he twisted and turned until he wrenched himself free, spitting all the while. Every now and then he stopped to listen and look about him, his eyes as big as the acorn that came plopping down out of nowhere and hit him on the nose. Once he came within an inch of colliding with a rabbit that was standing tall and white against a patch of old snow with a cross-stitch pattern of sunlight on him coming down from a break in the trees. The rabbit was twitching its nose, exploring possibilities, and took a jump away from him. Pinky arched his back, hissed menacingly, and ran a little faster.

Something kept calling him, telling him to go on. He did. Even if another cat had asked him what it was that told him to keep going, he would not have been able to tell him, though both would have known that the urge must be obeyed.

Finally he came to a spot where blacktop began, beyond a scraggly line of frost-stiff grasses and tangled vines. This was something new for him and he stopped and smelled the edge of the road carefully before putting his feet on it. The spot where he stood was directly opposite the Nickersons' house, and anyone looking out of one of its many windows might have spied Pinky crossing the road — once he had assured himself it was harmless — but there was no one at any of the windows and so Pinky walked across in leisurely fashion, unseen.

He clambered up the shoulder of land that lifted the Nickerson lawn from the level of the road. Tall grass beckoned to him, promising shelter from prying eyes, and he crossed the vast distance and went straight into it. Soon he was happily hidden from view. There was absolutely no use miaowing. He knew that now. He sat down and gave himself a thorough wash, which restored his confidence beyond description. In fact, it would have been impossible to tell anyone — save another cat — what this did for him. But as one cat to another, they would have agreed that it put the world right side up. After a while he was able to look about him and consider where he was, and he did it with the ease of a mighty king who knows that all he sees is his.

The Nickersons kept their small cabin cruiser bedded in the sand of the dunes, its deck slightly below the level of the lawn. There was a shed roof over it, but three sides were open to the weather. On the ocean side instead it was not only protected by boards neatly fitted and caulked which reached to the shed roof, but also had the additional safeguard of the stout tarpaulin, pegged down tight, which covered the whole boat. These precautions were necessary because, though safe in ordinary winter storms, there was a chance that high seas might reach the cruiser quite easily during the bad storms that come in spring and fall. These, which the natives call line storms, fall due almost without fail at the time of the equinoxes, and all up and down the Cape people keep a weather eye out for them.

As matters stood at the moment, a good stretch of dunes lay between high-water mark and the cruiser. The dunes were all humps and hummocks, with the ribs of an old shipwreck sticking out at one point, and poverty grass, the color of a lion's mane from late fall till spring returned, thatching the more sheltered spots. In summer bright pink roses grew there.

The sun flung a handful of gold on the shed roof now as it ended the day, saving most of it for a backdrop to the pine woods, the valley beyond them, and a distant cottage on a knoll back of that. A frosty breeze had begun to blow in from the far dunes in the direction of Nauset Light, black clouds were gathering there, and high overhead geese went honking south following their leader in wedge formation. It was the only sound in the deep quiet dusk.

Pinky, one delicate paw suspended in mid-air in the act of washing, looked at the gilded roof a short distance ahead of him. Some of the brightness touched the tarpaulin itself and he detected motion. It was the slightest flutter of one flap of canvas. Interest kindled into slow, cautious motion. His bony frame hardly shifted the blades of poverty grass, but now and then their covering of hoarfrost crackled too loudly for his sensitive ears. Then he remained as still as castaway drift-wood anchored in sand for an instant or two to cover his progress. Not a whisker moved. No older or more experienced cat could have beaten his stalking technique, which he must have known before his eyes were open.

A board led from the height on which Pinky stood to somewhere under the tarpaulin, and at this point the canvas was partly torn, which was the reason why it had moved when the breeze touched it. Smelling the board carefully inch by inch as he went forward, Pinky finally pushed his small, pale nose into the opening — then one eye — then the other — then his whole head. By slow degrees less and less of him was visible from the outside, until finally his tail disappeared entirely under the golden canvas.

One short leap downward and he had entered a warm and fragrant world. He could not himself have said that he smelled fish and mice, but that is what the fragrance was. He landed on something soft. Or, at least, it was softer than anything he had been on for some time. In a little valley of this new softness were three small, somewhat round objects which were warmer than the surrounding nest.

Pinky gave two or three experimental purrs,

started kneading, and, in a sudden wild burst of joy at having found a happy place, began sparring with one of the three warm objects. To his great surprise, it rolled over and fell with a distinct crashing sound below his perch. He peered down full of curiosity. The thing had broken and was spilling some liquid all around it, but the center looked round and more solid than the rest. Pinky fell more than leaped down, and having got both his paws wet, licked them. It tasted good. He settled himself down to lapping, and this time he did not shiver.

When he had finished, he looked for a way to climb toward the soft spot on which he had first landed and found a wooden slat that enabled him to get where he wanted to be. As he washed, his eyes pierced the dusky corners of his wonderful cavern. He burped happily and purred louder and still louder until his thin frame rocked with the sound. He blinked into the darkness which made everything pleasantly visible to him, and in the very act of giving himself an extra lick, he toppled over sideways and fell sound asleep.

6

Brad Nickerson wasn't going to kill that hen no matter what anybody said against her. He'd miss her if he did. He knew he would.

Mrs. Nickerson said, "She isn't laying *any* eggs, Brad. You mind what I say." When she saw that he was thinking his own thoughts on the matter, she said, "If you're so sure she's laying eggs somewhere, tell me where."

"Darned if I know, Liddie. But she's a young hen, it stands to reason she's laying eggs *somewhere*."

"I don't believe those summer people. She don't look old, I'll say that, but you can't tell. Why would anybody keep a chicken in an apartment in New York City, tell me that, Brad Nickerson?"

"I did tell you, Liddie, only you forgot. It belonged to their kid. He got her as a chick couple, three Easters back. Then he went to boarding school and they couldn't keep her 'cause they moved into a no-pet apartment or something of the sort. Seems they have freak rules like that in the city. Joe was the kid's name, nice lad, saw him once, said he wouldn't mind if he knew she was in the country with nice people. We're the nice people, see."

"Great! Well, you're paying for the feed, Mister. I've said my last say about that fool hen," Liddie declared and went to throw potato peelings into what they called their "feed pot" back of the stove. Later Brad would take it out to the little porker that lived on the other side of the barn. "As the old timers used to say," Liddie Nickerson continued, "scraps is cheap but what you buy at the store ain't."

When Brad walked into the barn there was the hen, speckled black and white and sassy. "You better tell me what you're doing with those eggs," Brad told her. "I can't stand much more jawin' on your account."

She cocked her head at him and said, "Cluck!" Then she walked toward him with measured steps to see whether he had any good ideas on food. It seems he had. He gave her a handful of corn from the pail he was carrying. Actually, she was more interested in visiting at the moment, so she hopped on one of his feet. He bent down, picked her up, and held her in the palm of his hand.

"Listen, Tock," he told her, "no more stalling, or we're in trouble, you and me." For some reason, a few days after he had taken her in, he had started calling her Tock, though the boy said her name was Ophelia.

Tock said, "Cluck!" And then as an afterthought, "Cluck, c-c-cluck!" and turned to look at him sideways.

"All right!" said Brad, just as if she had made him a promise. "See that you do."

He put her down and went about his chores. Tock followed him, stopping now and then to peck at things which only she could see, making a variety of small, contented sounds.

To Tock's way of thinking — chicken fashion to be sure — to lay an egg was strictly a private affair.

To this end she had finally worked out a plan. First she meandered down to the dunes as far from the cruiser as she could get, then she ran along under the shelter of the embankment until she reached it. Here she hopped on a low boulder close to the keel of the boat, and from it fluttered upward to the shelter of the poverty grass. As she walked on the board that led to the ripped spot in the canvas, she was completely hidden by the tall, stiff grass. All this was to her entire satisfaction and she found the cruiser much the best of many secret (and sometimes hazardous) locations in which she had been depositing eggs for the past three months.

When Pinky, on the first morning that he met Tock, heard one or two little pecks at the opening in the tarpaulin, he appeared to have received advance information that a friend was about to enter, and this was before he had even set eyes on Tock. He moved back noiselessly, settled himself with his paws neatly folded under him, and waited.

Tock came in, clucking softly to herself. After giving a few pecks at the cover she settled down to her work on top of the two round objects that were left. Without looking either to the right or to the left, she had not the least idea that a small cat was watching her. Her neck disappeared in her breast feathers, and her head came to rest comfortably on them.

Pinky studied her for a long time, and was certain that his advance information had been correct and that she was not only a friend but the marvelous creature who had left him something to eat the day before when he had first discovered the great cave. He approved her quietness, she looked soft — which was in anybody's favor — and she also had a pleasing voice and an excellent odor. But suddenly, as if an electric current had shot through him, Pinky was alert. A tiny creature no bigger than one of his paws was trying to get under Tock's feathers. With one masterful spring Pinky had it under his needle-sharp claws, and with a wretched squeak the thing grew limp as the claws dug into the tender flesh.

Tock said, "Cluck-cluck," with several nervous jerks of the head to emphasize disapproval, then she became fully aware of Pinky for the first time and said, "C-c-c-cluck!" irritably. She had long been acquainted with visiting dogs and cats and was on terms of friendship-with-dignity in both cases. The field mice that infested the boat had been Tock's only complaint about her new hideout, and now here was a friendly animal taking the nuisance away. It was fine.

Calmly, she went on laying her egg, while Pinky was getting his first taste of mouse.

7

This collaboration between Pinky and Tock soon progressed to the point where Pinky could nestle against Tock's deliciously warm feathers and enjoy a good sleep while she laid her egg, or he could merely sit. Tock would sometimes turn and give Pinky a few friendly pecks on the head, which made Pinky's ears twitch, though he never opened his eyes. Occasionally they sat together and talked in monotones of clucks and mews, and when Pinky purred, invariably Tock would jerk her head — as though he had surprised her — and give him a peck on the head. Once Pinky tried to wash Tock, but neither of them thought much of the idea.

Christmas had come and gone, and the lighted trees and stars and Santa Clauses and reindeers and all the other resourceful and inventive decorations which had lighted the roads and houses of the Cape were put away for another year. Heavy storms went howling up and down and eastways and westways, and shacks and boats that had sat on the bay side would be found like odd castaways on the ocean side come spring. Or the other way round. Thick ice floes lay all along the banks of the inlet back of Snow's Landing, and some of them even piled up on the harbor shore. There were days when the snow came down so thick and heavy that Cap'n Dan couldn't see his one-legged gull who came for slops each morning and sat himself on top of a telegraph pole directly across from Dan's usual window seat. But Sadie never failed to run out with the steaming slops for the bird. Her gray, skinny pigtails flying, she would clutch her heavy flannel robe with its silk cord and tassel swinging in the wind, since she usually did this in the early morning near breakfast time. By noon the slops would be gone, or they might be frozen solid to the tin plate, in which case Sadie would serve them up hot again next morning, sure that Cap'n Dan's gull wouldn't miss two meals in a row.

There were stormy times when Bill's truck went no faster than five miles an hour as he approached the dunes on Champlain Road. Even so, when he jumped out, if Doyle could see as far as the breadth of a couple of paws in front of his nose, he would go out and patrol the woods as usual. His brown and white long-haired tail played havoc with Bill's seat as well as his own. Bill was used to that, but he didn't much like it. "Hey, you, Doyle!" he would say, "You got my seat all wet. Keep on your own side." Doyle's reply was to give him a nudge on the sleeve and Bill never could figure out whether he meant, "I'm sorry," or "Get on with the driving, will you."

During those heavy snowstorms Liddie and Brad Nickerson, who had one of the clearest views across Nauset Harbor, the far dunes, and the horizon beyond them, could see no more than a foot beyond their windows. Likely as not the next day would be clear as water in a cup of white china, and the keel ridge of pines against the bluest of blue skies would look like a row of children with dazzling white mittens and caps ready for a long winter's tramp.

Heavy storms kept Tock away, and Pinky, who had grown accustomed to sallying forth on various cat errands each day, took courage enough to go out looking for her in the vicinity of the barn. How he knew she lived there is a mystery, or perhaps just wind-talk which he could explain simply to any who might understand. Anyhow, Pinky knew she lived there and he would sit himself somewhere out of sight and watch for a while.

Pinky wasn't always as out of sight as he thought he was.

"Looks like a rabbit there," Liddie said, watching Pinky stalking through the grass going in the direction of the barn. "Where are my glasses? I can't see so good that far."

"That's no rabbit." Brad's eyes were sharp. "That's a half-grown cat — more a kitten, as a matter of fact. Likely one of them wild ones from somewhere around. You know, Liddie, house cats never get as nice a coat of fur as these wild kittens. They live in a tree hole, or under an old house or barn, maybe, and their fur is as thick and glossy as if they slept in a feather bed."

"And sometimes they die," said Liddie. "Summer people!"

Brad, who knew summer people sometimes did leave their animals behind to shift for themselves, was nevertheless more tolerant of them.

He went on as if he had not heard her. "Look at that one, now. Sleekest, plumpest mite of a tiger cat I've seen in a long while. He does look like a gray rabbit — just a ball of fur."

"Eh-ya. You're right, Brad," Liddie agreed, looking at Pinky through her glasses now. "Golly, Brad, wouldn't Handy-Sandy love him though! That's a good-looking cat. Sandy was the one got done out of a kitten at the Christmas party. Remember?"

"I seem to remember something about Mr. Thomas objecting — kitten too scrawny, ugly, or something."

Liddie nodded. "Was Higginses' cat, too; everything a kitten shouldn't be — wouldn't live anyhow, that's what Mr. Thomas said, and there just wasn't another kitten to be had — always is, it seems, but there wasn't then. Handy-Sandy was so disappointed. I hear Sadie and Cap'n Dan got the poor thing a home anyhow. Must be dead by now if he was as bad as Mr. Thomas thought — just ribs, I remember."

"Don't touch the curtain, Liddie. Cat's eyes are mighty sharp. I want to see where he's going."

"Seems to be just sittin' far as I can see," said Liddie. "Must be darned cold sitting there."

"With that thick coat of fur! He can take it.

Prettiest cat I've seen in a long while — that bushy little tail. Might have some angora in him."

"Maine cats are as furry as that, aren't they?"

"Yes, that's true. And we do have quite a few around. You're right, Liddie, it would be great if we could get it for Handy-Sandy."

"Oh, Brad, he's making for the barn. Nice cat and all that, but you better go out there and chase him off. There's no telling about these wild cats. He's not very big, but you just don't know what they might do. I knew one who broke eggs like an expert cook — and ate them!"

"Well, unless he meanders toward the chicken coop, he won't have much chance to feast, with only Tock hanging around that barn now." Brad grinned at Liddie, never dreaming how well supplied in eggs Tock kept that very same "wild cat." He would have been surprised indeed to learn that Tock's production of eggs averaged nearly one a day, no matter what tricks the weather played on her.

"Can't you get that hen in the coop where she belongs?"

"She won't stay. She keeps getting back to the barn — likes it better, no doubt."

"Oh, pardon me!" Liddie laughed. "I forgot

she was a New York hen. No, I'm not saying a thing against *your* hen, Brad. I've written her off as *our* barn decoration."

"She might surprise us and lay an egg for Easter. As you say, Liddie, you never can tell."

"I'll need a gold plate to serve it on with the price we paid for it. You going to give that cat a holler before he gets to your precious hen?"

"Pooh," said Brad, apparently convinced that that cat out there was no menace to Tock or anything else in the barn. But he walked out and stood on the steps a minute. "Shoo!" he shouted at Pinky in a half-hearted manner. Pinky streaked out of sight, jumped down the embankment and investigated other possibilities for reaching Tock.

8

Liddie and Brad taught school at Orleans, Liddie the second grade, and Brad the fourth. Each had a special and interesting project going all the time. It changed of course, but it was more or less the same sort of project because it always had to do with *their* children, as they called them.

Handy-Sandy had been Liddie's special project since the Hollowe'en school party. Her real name was Hannah Snow, but people had been calling her Handy-Sandy since she was a tot no taller than a spool of thread, which was her mother's pet phrase. The fourth in a family of seven children, Handy was the only one who had got short-changed on looks. She was all of one color, it seemed, with long, narrow eyes that looked golden and rather nice in the sun, but at other times were just long and narrow. Every night she gave her lank, sandy hair one hundred strokes of the brush, counting them carefully, to the amusement of her brothers and sisters. Her hair certainly did shine, but that was all that could be said for it. She looked as clean as a snowflake, and as fragile, though her mother used to say, "I can count on my Hannah to stay on her feet when everybody else comes down with something." Her efforts to hold this advantage were little short of heroic at times. And it surprised no one that her mother, as everyone else, took this for granted.

People said that the sad part of it was that from the time she could walk and talk, almost, Handy-Sandy knew how poorly she compared with the rest of her family. But the sad part wasn't that at all. The sad part was that they thought it was sad and in some way or other managed to make Handy-Sandy aware of it. The more they made her feel that way, though, the more Handy-Sandy ran around doing things for people so that they would love her. She remembered what people wanted and went after it for them, she listened kindly to other children who were in trouble, she shared what she had without complaining, she fetched and carried for everybody who seemed to need it — and some who didn't. But instead of loving her for it, they thought her funny.

It was that way at home and at school, and anywhere. When they weren't amused they simply took her for granted. When they saw her going out of her way to deliver somebody else's library books, someone was sure to say, "Good old Handy-Sandy!" not in admiration or affection but with a slight snicker. The children at school would say without a second thought, "Oh, Handy-Sandy'll do that," and leave her to pick up all the crayons they had spilled. And Handy-Sandy did pick them up — without a murmur. What amused them most was just this, that she never complained and she never got mad at them, but went at whatever she was doing with a steady, dogged, unruffled pace. Johnny Harden, who was in her class, summed it all up. He said, "She's everybody's Handy," and you could see he didn't think much of that.

At the Hallowe'en party Liddie watched

Handy-Sandy fetch and carry for everybody, and now she and three or four other children had been left to clean up. Suddenly Handy pressed her fists to her mouth and moaned, "I am *dying*! I am *dying*!" in such a tone of agony that though Liddie had been expecting an outburst for some time, she was completely startled by the words. She knew of course that Handy wasn't dying, or even physically ill. She grabbed her hand and took her outside to a secluded part of the hallway. Squatting down so that they were both the same size, Liddie said, "Hannah Snow!"

"They don't love me." Handy looked like a ghost child to Liddie in that moment, the pale color of her hair almost the same color as her cheeks. She was trembling all over, but she wasn't crying. Liddie wished she would. It seemed better if she would.

"They don't love me no matter what I do! None of them do." Handy said it in a low, tight voice, as if there weren't enough breath to say it in. "There's nobody nowhere to love me."

It would have been easy for Liddie to go all tender and look sad, but that wasn't Liddie's way.

"Will I do?" she asked.

Handy shook her head.

56

"Pooh to you!" said Liddie.

Handy looked at Liddie steadily. Her lips were white but they were not trembling like the rest of her. "Pooh to you yourself!" she said with spirit.

That half-angry exchange between them made them giggle. Then they laughed. They laughed a little harder — and then they really laughed with a merry ring to their laughter until tears rolled down Handy-Sandy's face.

"Here's a handkerchief," said Liddie.

"Thank you," said Handy.

"Was pooh-to-me-myself the answer to my question?" Liddie asked.

Handy-Sandy threw her arms around Liddie and hugged her tight.

Liddie said, "My husband Brad has a hen named Tock. He's forever doing nice things for her and she doesn't even love him enough to lay him an egg."

"Why not?"

Liddie shrugged. "Who knows! Some hens are like that. Some people are like that. Don't you like doing things, Hannah?"

Handy nodded. "But I want the children to love me, too."

"Eh-ya" Liddie agreed. "Tell you what, let's strike a bargain, you and me."

"All right."

"Save half the things you would do for the children, to do for me instead. After all, I *do* love you."

"Do you really?"

"Cross my heart," said Liddie, crossing it. "Sometimes I'll ask for the half you've saved, and sometimes I won't, but you just keep that half for me. Now, that means you'll have to say 'no' to the others half the time. Think you can do that?"

"Yes, I can," said Handy earnestly.

"Let's shake on it," Liddie said.

They did.

That was how Liddie's project with Handy-Sandy started.

9

Along about spring one evening Sadie and Dan had gone to have a look on the ocean side. Dan stood in the doorway and Sadie stepped down the three porch steps to the little patch of seared grass below them.

There was a hint of new green among its yellow, and the bayberry bushes and beach plums that dotted the stretch of land back of the house had that indefinable look of promise composed chiefly of hope in the eye of the beholder. They were a long way from putting out buds. It was one of the first warm evenings they had had so far.

Even the setting sun had a spring look to it — so they thought — and was bidding them a pleasant evening with a shower of russet gold on their house and land. Sadie was holding up a hand against it, and she was thinking, as she nearly always did when she stood on this side of the house and looked out across Nauset Harbor, how much better it had all been when there were fewer trees. Then she could look way out to Kingdom Come across the dunes to Nauset Light. Well, it was pretty anyway.

"Look at who's lookin' at you, Sadie," Dan said.

"Where?" Sadie turned to look at Dan, who motioned with his chin the other way.

"Down by that juniper next to that old wooden tub that's been restin' there all winter. Don't move none or you'll scare 'em."

Sadie looked, and there was Pinky, sitting next to the tub and having a good look at them both. "Bless me, it's Pinky!" she said, taking less than a split second to recognize him.

"Eh-ya. Thought you'd know him. Got that same light streak across his nose. Kinda like a clown — only, nobody'd say he was homely now."

"And that there's the Nickersons' pet hen. Guess they took up together during the winter somehow."

"Real friendly," said Dan.

"Sure it's Pinky." Sadie sounded as if she were reassuring anyone who would disagree with that. "But, Dan, look at him! Would you believe it."

"Yes I would."

"Ain't he the handsomest little cat you ever laid eyes on? Now, Dan, what do you suppose happened to them Colby people?"

"No tellin', Sadie. Know that cat anywhere. He sure plumped out, though. Lord says, if you need to stay out the winter I'll give you an extra heavy coat. Maybe them people left."

"Could be. She hasn't been around since I gave her the cat."

"Told you we'd see him back, didn't I, Sadie?"

"You sure did!" Sadie called, "Pinky!"

Pinky's ears twitched but he continued to sit by the upturned tub looking at them.

Tock, who had been busily scratching and pecking close by, looked up and threw a few friendly sounds at the company round her.

"Stay where you are," Dan told Sadie, "and I'll fetch him some milk."

"Warm it a little," Sadie said, and sat down on the bottom step.

Tock looked up when Dan put the saucer down on the grass and in a minute took a headlong run toward it, then slowed down to a dignified walk

and looked at it, head to one side. But Pinky wouldn't budge. If Tock wasn't interested enough to try whatever it was, neither was he.

This performance was repeated on several evenings after that.

Then, rather suddenly, the weather worsened as if spring had been forgotten. Dan and Sadie did not open their back door for a few days. So many people were down with ailments of one sort or another and they had few callers. It was just as well to be careful. Most of their days were spent by the fire, as in winter. The chill of spring rains was every bit as bad as the cold of winter, even a little worse, and it might fool anyone into believing that less care was needed now. At least, that was the theory by which Dan and Sadie went, and so they did not open the back door at all and did not know that Pinky had been there on his own several wet and cold evenings.

He had walked around the house, investigating several mole tunnels, skunk holes, and a couple of woodchuck doorways. He had slunk under the low hedges that separated the house from the long, narrow, empty store next to it which Sadie had once run with both joy and profit, and he had given particular attention to the back and front doorsteps of the house itself. His conclusion was that these were the good guys.

One rainy evening, while Dan and Sadie were sitting close to the stove, they heard a plaintive mewing at the back door. It was Pinky. He was alone. When Sadie opened the door he retreated to the bottom step, dripping wet, and looked at her wistfully.

Sadie promptly forgot all her fine theories about damp spring weather, left the door half open, and went to get him a saucer of milk. When she set it down by the door Pinky looked at it as if it was of no interest to him, but he might have a look at it. With a few wet hops he reached the saucer and immediately began lapping up the nice warm milk, while Sadie squatted down watching him. Dan looked at them both from his seat by the fire.

After a while he said, "Wish you'd come in — both of you. That's mighty damp weather rolling in through that door."

It was almost as if Pinky understood him. He looked up, gave his whiskers a hasty lick and hopped on Sadie's lap.

Dan said, "That now is one of the prettiest compliments you ever got, Sadie."

Sadie's thin face glowed with pleasure as she stroked Pinky with one finger. "I always did have a way with wild things, and he's not even wild — he's Pinky." Pinky looked up at her and purred.

In a minute all three of them were sitting by the fire, Pinky on Sadie's lap, blinking at the flames, purring, occasionally stretching his neck toward one or the other of them as if he were going to say something, then purring louder still. There was no mistaking what he had to say to them. "This is what I was thinking of when I first came here. Remember? Long, long ago."

10

Handy-Sandy had been invited to stay with the Nickersons a whole month around Easter time.

One sunlit morning in late March, right after breakfast, Liddie and Handy-Sandy came upon Brad as he sat inside the cruiser counting egg shells.

"I've counted three dozen so far," he said, "and I think there are about a hundred too crushed to count — at least, it looks that way."

"Congratulations!" Liddie said. "So that's where Tock was laying her eggs! Well, you can say I told you so if you like."

"I wasn't going to say a thing." Brad continued to pile up egg shells.

"Then she did love him!" Handy-Sandy's face glowed with happiness.

Brad and Liddie exchanged glances and then looked at their young guest. They looked as happy as she did, because they knew that Handy-Sandy was beginning to know she was loved. And that was exactly what they wanted her to know and to be sure of.

"Yes, she did love him," Liddie said, as if it were the most natural thing in the world. "And Brad knew it all the time," she added, smiling at her husband.

"There's more love going around the world than you and I know about, Sandy. You just keep that in mind. I'm grateful for that love, Liddie, and I also want to congratulate the cat."

"What cat?"

"Oh, the cat that fattened on Tock's eggs, the cat that also saved our boat from being chewed to bits by field mice, the cat you saw that you thought Handy might like to have."

"Brad Nickerson, how do you know so much?"

"Well, Mrs. Nickerson, I get around you know, and I keep my eyes open."

"You're impossible!" Liddie said. "But if that enchanting, beautiful, charming cat who took up with Tock broke over a hundred eggs, let me remind you that fresh eggs were selling a dollar a dozen just about Christmas time."

"Glad to hear it." Brad looked up and grinned. "You certainly keep track of things yourself, Lydia Nickerson," he said, returning to his counting of egg shells.

"Why are you counting them, Mr. Nickerson?" Handy asked.

"Exactly what I was going to ask," Liddie said.

"That makes forty-two.... Just wanted to see how much of a fortune we could have made on Tock. Now here's a roundabout success story for you two. We break even. And you know why? If Tock hadn't been laying eggs here, the cat wouldn't have settled down to his happy home, and the mice would have chewed up everything in sight. As it is, only one small section of the seat has to be replaced."

"Well, cheers for the cat! Say, Brad, since we have contributed to that cat's support the better part of the winter — in a remote way, that is — why couldn't we try and get him for Hannah? If we can find him."

"He's all found, girl!"

Handy started jumping up and down. "Oh, Mr. Nickerson, he can take the place of the one I didn't get at the Christmas party."

"He *is* the one you didn't get at the Christmas party."

"He is? But — but they said he was sickly and wouldn't live!"

"I guess he used up one life, then. But he's got eight left. Liddie, I know you're perishing to know how I know so much."

Brad jumped out of the cruiser and came to stand beside them, wiping his hands on his overalls.

"When I went to the post office I picked up Dan's and Sadie's paper and stopped by to give it to them. Dan and Sadie both recognized him. He came to their house on several evenings until he satisfied himself they were old friends—or worthy of his trust, or something. Anyway, he's there. He had a light streak down the length of his nose."

"Yes, I remember that, Brad, because everybody said he looked like a clown. And he had a pink nose."

"That's why they called him Pinky I guess," said Handy-Sandy.

"Right." Brad looked down at the pointed, serious little face of Hannah Snow staring up at him wide-eyed. "And guess what Sadie said? She said we should go over there this afternoon and bring Hannah so she can meet *her own* cat."

"Oh, Mr. Nickerson!" Hannah Snow's joy didn't exactly spill into words, but it didn't have to. It was all in her face.

Liddie looked thoughtful. "I wonder what happened at the Colbys. They're still living in Brewster. I saw them driving by one day."

"Maybe he ran away."

Liddie shook her head. "Too small to know his way back here. He couldn't have been much more than six weeks when I saw him before Christmas time."

"I don't suppose we'll ever know," Brad said.

"How did they ever tame him when he was running around wild so long?"

"Didn't need any taming, Liddie. If you hadn't lived in Boston most all your life, you'd see the difference between real wild things and those that have only been left to themselves for a while. That little cat was born into a home where there were a nice bunch of kids, and he had tender loving care from birth to his sixth or seventh week. The Higginses are kind people. Whatever happened after he went to stay with the Colbys — as I said, we'll never know. And it don't matter now anyway."

"You're right, Brad."

"However it happened," Handy-Sandy said, "Pinky's come home." Between the sudden color in her cheeks and the sunlight which was catching the tawny light in her eyes and weaving pale gold in her long hair, she looked quite attractive. Liddie watching her with fond eyes thought that perhaps, like Pinky, she would one day grow very pretty.

"Of course, you won't be able to take Pinky home with you right away," Brad said.

"I know."

"You'll have to visit with him a while."

"And I can do that every day while I'm here."

"Dan and Sadie will love that, too," Liddie said.

"You know, Mrs. Nickerson," Handy said with that odd half-grown up composure that made her a striking little personality in her own right, "my mother said she wanted me to have that Christmas-stocking cat — said my little sister Connie and I could have him in our bedroom because it's downstairs and nearer to go out. So I'm sure it's all right."

"He's coming to you a bit late, but now he's hale and hearty and full of charm."

"And with a fascinating mystery about his return, too," Brad added, grinning.

About four o'clock Brad and Liddie and Handy-Sandy walked to Cap'n Dan's and Sadie's house, not taking the shortcut from their backyard, which was just at the turn of Champlain Road, but walking the short distance sedately along the road. It made them feel as if they were really going on a special and important visit — which it was, of course. There was a mist out to sea, but the air inland was clear and the land had a spring look in the late afternoon sun. Brad was carrying Tock under his arm, and both Liddie and Handy were wearing their best Sunday clothes. Handy's blue woolen frock had a broad band of white at the hem which showed beneath her three-quarter-length plaid coat.

As they knocked on the door Brad said, "Since they've lost their happy home together, Tock and Pinky, they haven't seen each other."

Certainly Tock and Pinky seemed pleased at the encounter, though they had seen each other on Pinky's visits to the outdoors. Pinky's great delight with the warmth of the fire and all the love and attention he was getting — not to mention the good food — could never keep him away from the beloved moorland that held such a wealth of interesting information for him. The salt sea air was in his whiskers to stay.

Now he jumped down from a little chest of drawers beneath the pendulum clock, and apparently he had a lot to say to Tock. But Tock wasn't for staying indoors at all and pecked at the door. Finally, she fluttered over to Brad's knee — as a nice, familiar spot — and hoped she might soon get out where she belonged. Pinky couldn't understand it. A house was a marvelous place to be in. He stood by Brad's feet looking up at his friend with a grieved expression.

"Only be a day or so before that cat's ready to make friends with all of you," said Cap'n Dan. "He's going to be a good friend to you," he told Handy.

"He's been a good friend to Mr. and Mrs. Nickerson all winter," Handy said. "If it hadn't been for Pinky, half a boat might have been eaten up."

"Field mice must have got in and chewed up part of one seat," Brad said in answer to Dan's questioning glance. "I guess if Pinky hadn't been

there they would have finished the job all round."

Liddie laughed. "I agree he paid his keep, Brad, but he'll have to be kept well fed and away from chicken coops for the rest of his days."

"Wasn't that nice of Tock to take such good care of Pinky all winter," Sadie said, rocking herself complacently back and forth. "Whatever happened with them Colby people I don't know, but Pinky found himself a good friend in Tock, thank goodness."

Handy bent down and stroked the kitten gently. He looked up at her, and she thought his eyes asked her who she was. "I'm Handy," she told him. "Hannah Snow's my real name."

"You just come every day and visit with him, until he gets to know you real good. Got a little doll's cap and put it on him today." Sadie looked pleased with herself. "And he never minded. Some cats like you to dress them up."

"I wonder if I can dress him up — oh, just a cap, maybe — and put him in my doll carriage," Handy said. "I don't play with dolls any more. I used to when I was young. But my little sisters do."

"If he gets to like you he'll never mind. Had a kitten once when I was about your size and he looked real sweet in a carriage. Dan used to come and sit on the porch and whittle — same as he does now — and he used to look at me wheeling him in that carriage and shake his head like he thought I was daft. He used to say I'd spoil him for catching mice."

"Turned out different somehow." Dan chuckled, remembering. "Best mouser her mother ever had."

All this time Pinky had been standing near Brad looking up at Tock. Suddenly he took a leap and landed on Brad's free knee. In a minute he'd tucked his paws under him and settled down with the air of a cat who means to stay put till things go his way. At that moment there came a knock at the door.

"Must be Mr. Thomas," Dan said. "Thought he'd be coming by today sometime."

It was Mr. Thomas and he was pleased to see everybody, including Handy-Sandy who had been such an understanding child at that Christmas party where she had lost out on the kitten. Then he spied Pinky who had taken refuge on top of the dresser once more.

"Now that's the kind of little cat I had in mind for you in the Christmas stocking — smaller of course. That one must be five, six months old."

"Just about."

"He's a picture!" Mr. Thomas said, sitting down. "You remember I had to refuse the one you offered me, Sadie — you and Mrs. Higgins — 'cause the poor little fellow looked like he wouldn't last the day."

"Eh-ya," Sadie rocked back and forth. "I re-member."

"Where did you get this one?"

"Oh, round and about."

"It certainly is a beauty. Looks like a Maine cat."

"Eh-ya," Sadie said again. "Could be. Lots of 'em around. Nice and long-haired like a Maine anyhow."

Liddie wanted to say something about the little-known breed of Maine cats, but she realized in time that Sadie and Dan would rather change the subject, and in a minute Dan made a rather determined effort to steer away from the subject of cats in general. He asked about the new chapel (of which he knew nothing whatever), knowing that it would engage Mr. Thomas' interest instantly. It did.

Sadie made them some tea and served it with gingerbread, which she asked Liddie to slice for her. The conversation became lively with Cape interests of one sort or another, not least the coming of spring weather. Pinky remained on the dresser, taking a dim view of this surplus of newness, while Tock continued to sit on Brad's knee.

Just before they all left together, Mr. Thomas again expressed his delight over the kitten and the fact that Handy-Sandy was getting one of her own at last.

"Handy-Sandy and Pinky," said Mr. Thomas, and laughed.

"*Sandy* and Pinky," Liddie said.

"Dan!" Sadie was looking out the window as their guests were getting into Mr. Thomas' car to drive the short distance to the Nickersons. "I was dying to tell him!" She turned and smiled at him.

Dan bent down to stroke Pinky who was sitting close by the warmth of the stove between his feet. "I knowed you was, Sadie. But I think we did right. It might have been disrespectful to the parson."

Sadie agreed. "Sometimes I wonder, Dan, if Pinky would have grown so good in a house all winter long."

Dan looked out the window at the indigo sky of evening. The car had gone, the road was solitary. A long way across the dark moorland the lighted window of a cottage stood out in the dusk.

"It don't hurt none to be overcomin'," Dan said.